Say Cheese!

CAROLYN DINAN

ff
faber and faber
LONDON · BOSTON

Bill sat down to breakfast and frowned at the table.

"You don't look very cheerful," said his mother. "Is anything the matter?"

"No," said Bill. "I'm just practising not smiling. I'm going to keep my face like this all the time now. Well, till after next week anyway."

"What for?" asked his father.

Bill opened his mouth a little.

"It's my teeth," he muttered. "Look at them."

"They look very nice to me," said his mother. "As long as you brush them."

Bill shook his head sadly. "I'm the only one in my class with teeth like this.

“Gavin has a tooth missing on the bottom.
Mikki has one missing on top.
Tim has teeth missing all over the place

and David has two big teeth
in front
and Becky has hardly any
teeth at all.
Even the little twins have
matching gaps.

I haven't got a single tooth missing anywhere, let alone any big new teeth. Just two rows of baby teeth. You won't catch me saying 'cheese' next week. I'm going to look like this."

Gavin came into school late that day.

"I've been to the dentist," he said importantly. "I had a very bad toothache, and Miss Collins had to take out my tooth. I've got it here in a matchbox. I thought we could put it on the Nature Table."

"Did it hurt, having your tooth out?" asked Bill.

"Not a bit," said Gavin. "And I got a badge too!"

The next morning Bill sat up in bed and cried.

"My tooth hurts," he moaned. "I've got a VERY BAD toothache . . . oooohh!"

Bill's mother looked in his mouth.

"I can't see anything wrong," she said, "but we'll take you to the dentist right away."

"Open wide," said Miss Collins, peering into Bill's mouth. "Which tooth hurts?"

"Ik'sh my miggle toof up ong top," spluttered Bill. "Dat one dere."

Miss Collins poked it and tapped it and shook her head.

"Looks fine to me," she said. "The one next to it is a bit loose, though. Maybe that's what's bothering you."

Bill pushed the tooth with his tongue. It didn't feel loose. He pushed it again, harder. It moved very slightly. Miss Collins lowered the chair.

"Jump down, Bill. Now, which badge would you like?"

"Did you really have a toothache?" asked Bill's mother when they got home. "Or did you want to have a tooth out, like Gavin?"

Bill went red.

"What a fuss you're making," said his mother kindly.

"I'm not making a fuss," Bill replied firmly. "I'm just not going to smile."

The next day was Saturday.

"Come on, Bill!" called Anna and Tom. "Dad's taking us to the Fun-fair."

"You can each choose a different ride," said their father as they ran into the fair-ground. "Bill first."

"Bumper cars!" shouted Bill. "Please, Dad, they're the best. I'll drive. I'm good at driving."

"Don't forget these are Dodgem Cars, not Bumper Cars," said his father. "You have to try NOT to hit anyone."

But Bill wasn't listening.

12

Bang!

"Owww!" wailed Bill. "My tooth, my tooth!"

"Let's see," said his father anxiously. "No, it's all right."

"It's not all right," said Bill, cheering up suddenly. "It's all loose and wobbly. I bet it will fall out before we get home."

But it didn't.

All that weekend the tooth got looser and looser. Bill couldn't stop fiddling with it. He pushed it with his tongue so it stuck straight out in front. Then he sucked it back again and twisted it. Then he twisted it around so it was back to front.

"Stop it, Bill," groaned Anna. "Wiggle woggle all day. Leave it alone. It makes me feel sick to watch you."

"I've got an idea," said Tom. "Sit here, Bill. We'll tie one end of this piece of thread around your tooth and tie the other end to the door-knob."

"Now, keep still," said Tom. "I'm going to count three and then slam the door. ONE . . .
TWO . . ."

"AAAAAHHHHH
. . ." went Bill.

"That's bad," said Tom. "The thread broke."

"It's lucky it did," said his mother. "Don't you dare try that again. You could have hurt Bill."

"They did hurt me," grumbled Bill. "My tooth will probably fall right out after that."

But it didn't.

"I'm sorry, Bill," said Tom. "You can borrow my bike to make up."

So Bill put on Tom's crash-helmet and jumped on the bike.

"Look at me!" he shouted. "Watch, everyone. I can go on one wheel."

"Look out!" yelled Tom.

But it was too late.

Crash!

"OWWWWW!" howled Bill. "My tooth. Ooooohhhh!"

"Bad luck!" said Tom. "It's still there."

"Only just." Bill felt it with his finger. "It's hanging by a little bit of string. I bet I could pull it out easily."

But he couldn't.

It was still there next morning.

"Only one more day," sighed Bill.

"One more day to what?" asked his mother.

But Bill wouldn't say.

That evening, as Bill was going to bed, the doorbell rang.

It was Daisy, from next door.

"I've been cooking," she said. "I've made some brownies. Have one, Bill."

"Thanks." Bill took the biggest and bit into it. It was very hard and very chewy. He soon wished he had taken a smaller one, for his jaws were stiff from chewing. Suddenly his mouth felt funny.

He took out the bit of brownie. There, stuck into the top of it, was a little white tooth.

"It's my tooth," shouted Bill. "Come and see! Daisy got it out with her brownie."

Daisy smiled modestly.

"I'm going to be a dentist when I grow up," she said.

"That tooth came out just in time," said Bill next morning.

"In time for what?" asked his mother.

"I know," said Anna.

"We can wash my hair before school if you like," said Bill. "And I'll wear my best shirt today too."

"I know why Bill wants to look nice," said Anna.

"Don't tell Mum," begged Bill. "I want it to be a surprise."

And it was.

"It's good, isn't it?" said Bill proudly. "We shouted CHEESE so loud the camera nearly fell over."

"It's too bad you didn't keep your mouth shut," said Anna.

"It's lovely." Bill's mother gave him a hug. "I'll put it in a frame so everyone can admire it."

And that is what she did.